FRANCESCA CAVALLO

ELVES

on the Fifth Floor

Illustrations by Verena Wugeditsch

EDITORIAL DIRECTOR: Francesca Cavallo
TEXT: Francesca Cavallo
ILLUSTRATIONS: Verena Wugeditsch
GRAPHIC DESIGNER: Francesca Pignataro

Elves on the Fifth Floor is published by Undercats, Inc., a
small, independent publisher with a big mission: radically
increase diversity in children's media and inspire families to
take action for equality.

To see more of our books and download bonus materials and
free stories, come visit us at www.undercats.com

Printed in Canada

At Undercats, we do our best every day to minimize our
carbon footprint. We printed this book using FSC® certified
materials only, and we always make sure to print at plants
that are close to our distribution centers to reduce carbon
emissions due to transportation.

Dearest Readers,

It is with great joy that I welcome you to the city of R.

In a few pages, you will discover this wondrous city for yourself, as you explore its snowy streets with the Greco-Aidens. But first, let's talk, you and I.

Christmas is my favorite time of year. I come from a very big family, and every year since I was born, we have celebrated the holidays together. As a child, I loved watching the families in Christmas movies on TV, then turning around and looking at my own family around me.

However, as I grew up, I discovered that I wanted to build a family with another woman rather than a man; and in none of those Christmas stories could I find a family like the one that I hoped to start. I began to worry.

I would have liked to have shared my concerns with someone, but I believed that there must be some kind of secret reason why families with two mothers weren't in the stories I was reading, and I was too ashamed to ask *any* questions. I thought it was something I could do nothing about.

Today, I know there is a lot that each of us can do (yes, even kids!) to create a better world, a world where everyone is welcome and no one has to hide any parts of themselves.

The characters in *Elves on the Fifth Floor* are far smarter than I was as a child! Just like the young activists of our time, from Malala Yousafzai to Greta Thunberg, these children never stop asking, "Why?" They disobey adults' senseless rules, and in doing so, they change the world.

If I could go back in time, I would like to go back to my grandmother's bedroom, snuggle up with my sister and cousins, and read *Elves on the Fifth Floor* while the adults play cards in a nearby room on a long, green-cloth-covered table.

My wish is that this magical adventure keeps you and your families company during the holiday season, and that the courage of this exceptional group of children helps you be more accepting and feel more accepted.

With love,
Francesca Cavallo

For all the children
who disobey;
and, in doing so,
change the world.

This Way Street

ARRIVAL IN THE CITY OF R.

It was three days before Christmas when the Greco-Aiden family arrived in the city of R. There were five of them: two moms, Isabella and Dominique, and their three children, Manuel, Camila, and Shonda.

Tired from their long journey, the Greco-Aidens climbed down from the train car. They were about to head to the top of the platform when suddenly a little girl sped toward them—riding atop a suitcase that seemed to be motorized—until she crashed directly into the Greco-Aidens' luggage.

"Olivia!" A woman's voice called from far off.

Isabella and Dominique raced toward the little girl, Olivia. "Are you all right? Did you hurt yourself?" they asked, worried.

"No, thank you! Everything is exactly where it should be!" Olivia said, cheerfully brushing the dust from her jacket.

Shonda was entranced by the strange suitcase that Oliva had ridden in on. "What is that?" she asked.

"It's a Motocase," Olivia said proudly. "I built it myself." She watched the Greco-Aidens for a moment, then asked, "You aren't from around here, are you?"

"No," Manuel said. "We just got here. We're moving."

"And where are you going to live?" Olivia asked.

"Ten Roomy Chimneys Road. Do you know it?"

"Sure," Olivia said, whipping a map out of her pocket and pointing out a winding little road next to the station. "It's very close to the station. See? There's New Arrivals Square, and here's Roomy Chimneys Road, just to the right."

"Olivia!" It was the same woman who had called her before. "How many times do I have to tell you not to talk to strangers?" Without introducing herself, the woman grabbed Olivia by the arm and dragged her away.

"Welcome!" Olivia called over her shoulder, as she

disappeared after her mother into the crowd of travelers. Still reeling from the strange encounter, the three Greco-Aiden kids and their mothers started walking toward the station exit.

What they saw outside took their breath away.

The city of R. was beautiful!

Even though it was a cloudy winter day, the colors of the building facades sparkled like a rainbow after a thunderstorm: pink, canary yellow, blue, and aquamarine. The school holidays must have already started, for the streets were filled with children and their parents. The three siblings watched two dads chasing a little girl as she skated around an ice rink. Across the street, a mom, a dad, and their small twin children ran into a toy store. A mom and her three daughters—all bundled up in wooly scarves—perched on a green bench munching on steaming roasted chestnuts.

On the wall behind the bench was a huge poster. It was the only thing in New Arrivals Square that was not colorful. On the poster was a giant portrait of a man. He was thin and grizzled, with a tight-lipped smirk. One side of his mouth turned up as if to smile, while the other turned down into a frown. The man on the poster wore a dark gray suit, a light gray shirt, and a medium gray tie.

Printed below the picture in enormous letters was, *"NEW RECORD: NOTHING BAD HAS HAPPENED IN THE TOWN OF R. FOR FIVE YEARS!"* The message was signed, "Merry Christmas from Mayor Dull."

"What a peculiar name!" Camila said with a laugh, as she hurried to catch up with her family. They'd found the winding road Olivia had pointed out on the map: Roomy Chimneys Road, where their new home awaited.

Trudging under the mountain of luggage, bags, and backpacks, the Greco-Aidens found their way to Number 10. The facade of the building curved around the street corner. It was painted a bright orange, but in many places the plaster had peeled back, revealing the red bricks below. The three kids looked up, counting the windows above until they reached the top row. Number 10 Roomy Chimneys Road had five floors, and the Greco-Aidens' new home was on the top floor, the fifth.

THE HOUSE

The Greco-Aidens counted 104 steps on the climb to their landing. The door opened with a squeak, and the children rushed in while the moms wrestled with the luggage.

The truth was, there wasn't much to see: the apartment was small and bare. The kitchen was on the left; to the right, there was a small dining room with an old table and five spindly-legged chairs. The only big thing in the house was the fireplace, in front of which sat an iron poker and a basket filled with wood on an old carpet. There were two windows in the dining room: a large one on the wall and a small dormer window between the big wooden beams of the ceiling. A layer of ice had formed on the dormer window.

Manuel blew air into his hands to warm them up and watched as his breath puffed into a little cloud.

"Let's light the fire right away!" Camila, the most excited of the three, suggested. "I've always dreamed of having a house with a fireplace, and luckily we have plenty of wood!"

"Let's finish bringing in the luggage, then we'll light it," said Mama Dominique, as she attempted to drag in a large powder blue suitcase with worn-out wheels.

At the back of the dining room, a cream-colored door with a rust-spotted brass doorknob led to the only bedroom. Squished inside were a double bed, two straw stools that served as bedside tables, a small wardrobe, and a three-story bunk bed. All the furniture was lopsided, and there were no sheets or blankets on the mattresses.

"What do you say we all sleep together in the big bed?" Mommy Isabella asked. "That way, we'll all stay toasty warm!"

"Hurray!" Shonda cheered. In their old house, she had loved to sneak out of her room at night to snuggle with her moms in their big bed.

Isabella, Dominique, and the children came from a faraway country that had recently elected a new president. He had declared that families like theirs—ones with two moms and three kids—were illegal. The Greco-Aidens had fled in a hurry: otherwise, Manuel, Camila, and Shonda would have been sent to an orphanage, and their moms to jail.

"What does it mean that we are illegal now?" Camila had asked when they had read the news.

"I don't want to go to a *Forphanage*!" At four years old, Shonda had never heard the word "orphanage" but she had sensed that it might be hiding something unpleasant.

"Of course not," Mommy Isabella had reassured her.

"Nobody's going anywhere alone," Mama Dominique had chimed in. "Wherever we go, we'll be together."

So, they had packed their bags, said goodbye to their city and friends, and left for R.

Now, in the apartment on Roomy Chimneys Road, Manuel looked out the window and worried: "It's going to be hard at the beginning, not knowing anybody."

"We just met Olivia!" Camila reminded him, as she

helped Mama Dominique to light the fire in the fireplace. Camila could stay positive through anything. She was two years younger than Manuel, but she loved new challenges.

"She seemed nice…" added Shonda, a little doubtfully, as she pulled her teddy bear out of her backpack and tucked it carefully in a tiny, striped sleeping bag.

"And anyway," Camila went on confidently, "you saw that poster in front of the station. Nothing bad *ever* happens here!"

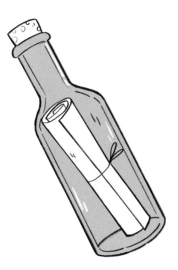

NEIGHBORS

Nothing bad ever happened in the city of R. The city was world-famous for it. In fact, it was for that very reason that Isabella and Dominique had chosen R. as their family's new home.

What they didn't know but would soon find out was that—much like Olivia's mother—the inhabitants of the city were not very friendly. When Isabella, Dominique, and the children rang the neighbors' doorbell to introduce themselves, nobody opened the door.

"Why aren't they coming out, Mommy?" asked Shonda, confused.

"Maybe no one is home..." Isabella replied hesitantly.

"But I saw an eye peering through the peephole!" Shonda protested.

"What if they don't want us here?" Manuel asked, worried.

"No way!" Camila protested. "They're just busy getting ready for the holidays!"

"Camila's right," Mommy Isabella cut in. "How about we get into the holiday spirit too? Who wants a nice hot chocolate?"

Excited, the Greco-Aidens hurried down the 104 stairs and down the street to the nearest cafe.

Imagine their surprise when at a nearby table they saw an old lady, accompanied by the same little girl whose motorized suitcase had nearly run them over at the station: Olivia!

"Hi, Olivia!" Shonda smiled at her.

The girl twisted toward Shonda and broke into a wide grin. She was about to say hi in return when the old lady —her grandmother, perhaps—froze her with a glare. Olivia immediately turned away and stared down at her bottle of blueberry juice.

Manuel, Camila, and Shonda looked at each other, puzzled. Perhaps the little girl was in trouble for the business with the suitcase? Well, they didn't want to get her into more trouble, so they went and sat down at another table.

When the waiter came to take their order, Dominique told him, "Good evening!" The man did not respond. He didn't even raise his eyes. He just kept staring down at the pen pointed at his notebook, waiting, until a confused Dominique ordered five hot chocolates. A few minutes later, the waiter placed the cups on the table and left without a word.

What was happening? Isabella and Dominique exchanged a look. Why wasn't anybody talking to them?

Olivia's grandmother got up to go and pay, but her granddaughter hung a few steps back. The little girl then casually swept past the kids, but as she passed by, she slipped her juice bottle onto their table. It was empty—except for a piece of rolled-up paper stuck carefully inside.

As she joined her grandmother at the counter, Olivia turned and winked at the Greco-Aidens, who stared back, open-mouthed.

"There's a message in the bottle!" Shonda whispered

to her siblings. Manuel and Camila exchanged a glance, and as soon as Olivia and her grandmother were out the door, Camila flipped the bottle upside down and fished the paper out with her finger.

It was the size of a bus ticket, both sides covered in dense writing. After carefully smoothing it out on the table, all five Greco-Aidens—including Shonda, who still did not know how to read—craned their necks to see what it said.

I'm so sorry for not saying hi! In R., the adults don't talk to strangers, because when you meet a stranger, unexpected things can happen, and Doctor Dull says that the only way to keep anything bad from happening in R. is to be careful not to let anything happen at all. But I love surprises, and you all seem very nice! I can't talk to you when there are adults around, but you can find me and other kids on the citizens band radio, on channel 38B.

The note was signed with an O, below which Olivia had drawn two small circles that looked like wheels.

"Who on earth is Doctor Dull?" Mommy Isabella asked.

"The mayor of R.," Camila replied, remembering

the huge poster she'd seen in the square that morning.

"What is the 'citizens band radio?'" asked Shonda.

The children and Mommy Isabella shook their heads. They had no idea.

Mama Dominique spoke up: "It's a CB radio," she said. "By choosing the same channel, two people can communicate with each other. My brothers and I used one years ago, when we were playing on opposite sides of a hill."

"Like a telephone?" Manuel asked.

"Not really," Dominique replied. "On the telephone, everyone can talk at once. On a CB radio, you have to be patient and wait until the other person has finished."

After a moment she went on, "But I didn't know that 'B' channels even existed. It must be an underground channel."

The children's faces lit up. "Maybe we could change the letter we wrote to Santa Claus and ask if he could bring us a radio as a present," said Shonda. Her siblings nodded.

Indeed, that was the very first thing they all did as

soon as they got back home. There were only two days until Christmas, and they didn't know if the letter would arrive in time for Santa Claus to switch the present. Still, they decided it was worth a try, so they wrote their letter and handed the envelope to Mommy Isabella to mail.

The first day in R. had brought more surprises than they could ever have imagined, yet the events of the day were nothing compared to what would soon take place on the fifth floor of Number 10 Roomy Chimneys Road.

THE NEW JOB

On the morning of December 23rd, Isabella went to the central post office in R. for her first day of work. She'd been hired as a mail carrier. When she got there, she found a heavy, brown leather bag bulging with mail to be delivered by bicycle around the city. With a map in one hand, and the handlebars in the other, Isabella rode around R., neighborhood by neighborhood, delivering greeting cards, magazines with shiny covers, small packages, invitations, books, and envelopes of every kind.

Isabella had been delighted to find this job. "I will meet lots of people, for sure!" she had told Dominique.

But her first day was a disappointment: every time she rang a doorbell to deliver the mail, the recipient

would appear in the window and motion nervously for her to leave it on the doorstep or the mailbox, or to slip it under the door.

"It's exactly like Olivia wrote in her note," Isabella said to herself. "They must be avoiding me because I'm a stranger."

At seven o'clock in the evening, she had finally reached the end of her route when she was dismayed to discover one last envelope in the bottom of her mailbag. The envelope was pink, addressed in blue ink, with old-fashioned handwriting, elegant and full of flourishes. One corner bore a golden stamp and an illegible postmark. Isabella was exhausted; it had been a long day, and she was past ready to get home. She read the address, hoping that it wasn't too far, and was surprised to read the name of her very own street—indeed, her very own building! How lucky!

And the recipient? She squinted to make out the three names on the envelope: Manuel... Camila... and Shonda?! Her own children!

Stunned, Isabella looked for the sender, but the

return address was too faded to read.

Who could have sent it? They had only just moved—their friends and family didn't yet know their new address. Even though she was burning with curiosity, Isabella decided that the right thing to do was to let the recipients open the letter themselves.

When she got home, she was greeted by the deliciously familiar smell of her wife's vegetable soup.

"My love!" Dominique lit up as she saw Isabella walk in.

"Hi, Mommy!" The children called out, hugging her.

"Hello, darlings!" Isabella said. "What have you been up to today?"

"We went grocery shopping at the market, hooked up the new phone, and helped Mama make dinner!" Camila said. "Manuel squashed a tomato on his face!" She giggled.

"Everyone to the table!" Dominique said, dishing the soup into the bowls.

"The dining car is about to depart!" Isabella called out and the children all hopped aboard. Manuel hung from her shoulder, Camila from her arm, and Shonda clung to

her leg as she huffed and puffed like a steam train loaded up with precious cargo. This was a favorite game of the Greco-Aiden family—and one that ensured that everyone reached the table at the same time, while dinner was still hot.

"Kids," Isabella announced as she sat, "I have a surprise for you!"

Dominique smiled and shook her head. Every so often, Isabella forgot that dinner time was not the best time to share surprises with the children— they would get distracted and not finish eating.

"What is it?" they all demanded, food forgotten.

"First, we'll finish our dinner," Dominique said, with a wink at Isabella, "then we'll hear what this is all about, okay?"

The children all picked up their spoons and wolfed down the hot soup as fast as they could. "Finished!" they announced a few minutes later, showing their empty bowls to their moms.

Mommy Isabella nodded in approval. "Now you just have to wait until we've finished, too!"

"Hurry up, Mommies!" the kids protested.

As soon as everyone had finished, Dominique solemnly declared, "Drumroll, please!" Each member of the family began to drum their hands against the tabletop. Mommy Isabella slowly wiped her mouth with her napkin. She loved drawing out the suspense.

"Today," she began, "after delivering all the mail, I found a letter addressed to some very special recipients. It was stuck to the bottom of my bag—hidden."

"Who was it for, Mommy?" Little Shonda asked, her eyes sparkling.

"Well..." Isabella pulled the envelope out of her jacket pocket and cleared her throat. "This letter is for... Manuel, Camila, and Shonda Greco-Aiden! Do you know them, by any chance?"

"That's us!" Manuel shouted, yanking the pink envelope from Isabella's hands.

He had begun to clumsily tear open the edge of the envelope when Camila plucked it out of his grip.

"Careful, don't rip it!" she protested.

With the authoritative air of a specialist, Camila delicately teased open the corner of the envelope, and pulled out an ivory-colored sheet of paper. She handed it to her brother. Of the three of them, he was the best reader.

"Whose is it? Who sent it to us?" Shonda asked excitedly.

Manuel began to read out loud:

"Dear Manuel, Camila and Shonda, This is..."

He paused and his eyes widened:

"This is SANTA CLAUS!"

THE FLYING ENVELOPE©

"Did Santa Claus answer our letter?" Shonda asked breathlessly.

Manuel read on: "I received your letter, even though it was sent last-minute. I'm proud to report that the North Pole Postal Service (NPPS) has greatly advanced in the last few years.

"Thank you for the kind things that you wrote in your letter, both Mrs. Claus and I appreciate it very much. I cannot tell you whether or not you will get the gift you asked for—that must remain a surprise!

"From your letter, I have come to understand that you recently moved to the city of R. Mrs. Claus and I would therefore like to ask a favor of you: Would you be so kind as to lend us a hand in wrapping the presents for the children in your new city?"

"Every single one?" Dominique wondered, exchanging a concerned look with Isabella.

Manuel went on, never taking his eyes off the letter: "If you and your mothers agree, tomorrow I will send ten elves to your house so you can get straight to work."

"Tomorrow?" Isabella was alarmed.

"Ten?" Shonda was thrilled.

Manuel read calmly on: "The envelope in which I sent your letter is a Flying Envelope©, the latest and most advanced invention to come out of the NPPS, designed for the most urgent of correspondence. You may reply by writing your response and inserting the sheet back into the same envelope you received.

"Warm Regards, Santa Claus."

As soon as Manuel finished reading, he put down the letter and looked up at his family, who stood speechless.

Had they really received a letter from Santa Claus? the children wondered. Or was it some kind of prank? How could Santa have answered so quickly during what were surely the busiest days of his year?

The moms, on the other hand, were thinking: *How can we possibly wrap so many gifts, in a house this small, in so little time?*

Little Shonda was the only one who wasn't concerned. She picked up Santa's letter and clasped it tightly to her heart.

In the meantime, Manuel and Camila were passing the pink envelope back and forth. Santa Claus had called it a 'Flying Envelope©'. They examined it carefully, but it didn't seem to be particularly special. When gently tossed in the air, it didn't take flight, but instead landed softly on the tabletop, just as any other envelope might have done.

Shonda was the first to break the silence. "Shall I get a sheet of paper so we can write back?"

"What do you want to say?" Dominique asked.

"That we agree! You can't possibly say no to Santa Claus!" Camila replied in a rush.

"Of course you can say no to Santa Claus," Isabella replied.

"You can say no to anybody when you don't want to

do something," Mama Dominique added.

"But I want to see the elves!" Shonda said.

"But where will we put them?" Manuel said, looking around with concern.

"Santa Claus knows where we live," Camila cut him off decisively. "If he asked us, he surely has a solution in mind."

Meanwhile, Shonda came back to the table with a sheet of paper and a pen.

"Write," she ordered Manuel, handing him the pen. "Dear Santa Claus," she dictated, "we thank you very much for responding to us so quickly. If we get the radio for Christmas we'll be very happy, but either way we want to help you wrap the presents for the children of R. Our home is small, but if you would like to send us your elves, I promise that we will do our very best to help."

The three children signed the letter—Shonda had only just learned to write her name—then Camila folded up the sheet of paper, stuck it in the envelope, and sealed it.

As soon as she had finished running her forefinger along the top edge, the envelope came to life. It lifted up in the air, hovered above the old table, and turned around. On the back of the envelope, the return address, which until that point had been too faded to make out, suddenly darkened:

Santa Claus - North Pole - HO HO HO

Before everyone's astonished gaze, the letter flew even higher in the air, reared back as though gathering force, then swiftly slid out through the bottom of the big window. It headed north, leaving the cold attic behind.

For a moment, the Greco-Aiden children were too stunned to do anything. Then, they rushed toward the window, but the speedy letter was already out of sight.

THE INVESTIGATION

When it was time for bed, Mama Dominique usually had to convince the children to brush their teeth and put on their pajamas. But not that evening: Manuel, Camila, and Shonda couldn't wait to talk about everything that had happened. They were ready for bed in record time and raced into the bedroom, shutting the door behind them.

They snuggled together tightly under the covers, but they had no intention of going to sleep. Instead, they stared at each other, waiting to see who would be the first to speak.

Manuel scratched the back of his neck and whispered, "Why do you think Santa Claus asked *us* for help? We don't know anyone here, we just moved."

"He might have asked someone else," Camila broke in.

"He might have..." Manuel echoed, with the air of a detective mulling over a particularly challenging quandary.

"Could someone have said *no* to him?" Shonda was shocked at the thought. She had smuggled in a small flashlight, and she punctuated her question by pointing its beam at her siblings.

"Think about Olivia's message," Manuel said. "Would the citizens of R. let ten strangers into their homes to wrap tens of thousands of presents for more people they didn't know?"

"That's true," Camila said. "Other kids' parents would never have agreed!"

"That's the reason Santa Claus wrote to us," Shonda exclaimed. "We are his only hope."

At that, everyone fell silent, lost in thought. Then Shonda asked, her eyes wide, "We won't let him down, will we?"

The three children shook their heads vigorously and promised that no matter what, they would complete the

mission that had been entrusted to them by Santa Claus.

At that very moment, the door handle began to turn down. The three siblings switched off their flashlight, laid down, and pretended to be sleeping, hands linked tightly beneath the covers. The second day in R. had been very exciting, but it was late, and the children were exhausted, so it wasn't long before they fell asleep for real.

THE MORNING OF CHRISTMAS EVE

When the children woke up on the morning of December 24th, it seemed as though Santa Claus's letter must have been a dream. It had snowed all night long, and the city of R. was so silent that it appeared to have been emptied of its inhabitants. Dominique was making breakfast when Isabella came out of the bedroom already wearing her postal carrier uniform.

"Good morning, Mommy," the children greeted her sleepily.

"Good morning," Isabella said, as she slipped on her rubber boots.

Today, she would have to get to work early. As any postal carrier knew, Christmas Eve was the busiest day of the year.

"I wonder if our letter made it to the North Pole?" Shonda mused.

"It snowed a lot," Manuel said as he stared out the window. "Maybe the envelope got wet and was too heavy to fly."

"If the envelope is the latest and most advanced invention of the North Pole Postal Service," Camila observed, "it will have been designed to travel in the snow..."

Her siblings nodded their heads in agreement as they dipped their favorite flower-shaped cookies in milk.

Dominique gave them each a little chocolate. "This is to celebrate Christmas Eve!" she said with a smile.

The children's faces lit up. "Happy Christmas Eve, Mommies!" they exclaimed in unison, and immediately began unwrapping their chocolates.

Every time one of their moms gave them a chocolate or a candy, they raced to see who could eat theirs first. This time, Camila won.

Isabella and Dominique toasted their daughter's victory by clinking their coffee cups together. "May this Christmas be magical for all of us and may the city of R.

be filled with love and happi-
ness!" Isabella cheered. Then
she kissed her kids and wife
and opened the door to leave.

"Have a great day, Mommy!"
the three children said between
mouthfuls.

"You too, my loves!" she said as she walked out to
the landing.

She was about to close the door when she looked
down the stairwell and froze.

"What's wrong?" Dominique asked, worried.

Isabella lowered her voice to a whisper, "It looks
like we have... guests."

In a split second the children rushed out the door
and onto the landing, pushing past each other to look
down.

They could hardly believe their eyes. A team of
smiling elves had formed a chain up and down the stairs
of the building and were passing boxes of every shape and
size from hand to hand. They wore green cloth coats and

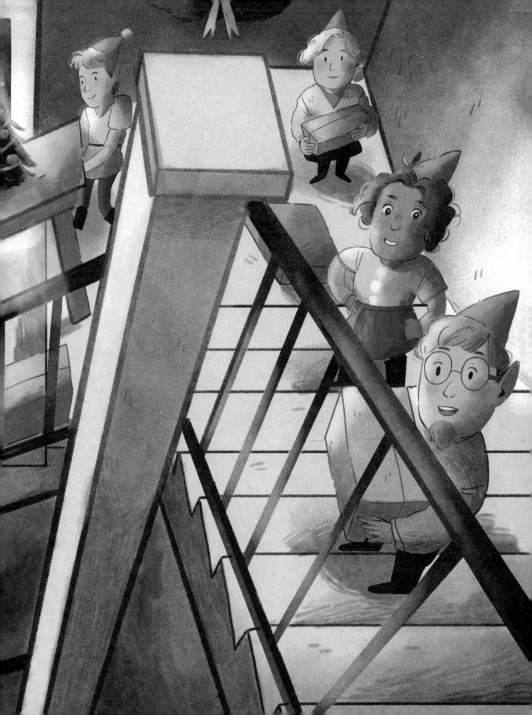

red cone-shaped hats, from below which their pointed ears emerged. Two of them were carrying a long, wooden table, piled high with more boxes, a Christmas tree, and even a tiny elf!

The stairs, which had up until then seemed so cold and bare, were now bursting with Christmas cheer. The elves had hung wreaths, bows, and stars on the walls. From the two windows, an enchanted light filtered in, filling the room with a magical glow.

"Oooh!" Shonda could not hold back her wonder.

Upon hearing the little girl, the elves put down their boxes and turned as one to look up.

TEN ELVES

The elves introduced themselves one by one.

"I'm Robert," the first greeted.

"My name is Romina!" the second said.

"I'm Rudy," said the third.

"Nice to meet you! Raphaëlle!" the fourth introduced herself.

"Raynold," came the fifth.

"And I'm Rachel," added the sixth.

"Hi, I'm Roy!" said the seventh.

"Pleased to meet you—Rose," the eighth smiled.

"My name is Rowan," followed the ninth.

"And I'm Roxanne," the last one concluded.

There were ten of them—just as Santa Claus had written in his letter!

Isabella and Dominique were speechless. The elves got right back to work, and before the Greco-Aiden family could rub their eyes to make sure they weren't dreaming, the apartment was full to the brim with packages!

Two days ago, that same apartment had barely been able to hold all their luggage. Now, it seemed to grow larger with every package that was brought inside.

Each box was carefully labeled: tape, bows, wrapping paper, means of transport, dolls, building sets, musical instruments, books...

Manuel, Shonda, and Camila were wandering among the boxes reading the labels when Raphaëlle and Rowan passed by carrying the long wooden table that, just as in the fairytales, not only managed to fit perfectly through the doorway but to everyone's astonishment, was just the right size for the room.

The two mothers remained speechless and kept looking back and forth at each other, The children were stunned, too, but they appeared to be having a lot of fun.

When the nearby church rang the nine o'clock bells,

Isabella winced. "I'm late!" she exclaimed. "I can't be late on my second day of work. Goodbye, my love!"

"And, well... good luck!" she added as she rushed out the door. Before Dominique could even say "goodbye," Isabella had disappeared down the stairs and toward the post office.

Dominique was doing her best to stay calm.

"Why don't you send the gifts directly from the North Pole?" she asked Romina, the elf who was setting up the long table where the presents were to be laid out.

"Up until last year," Romina explained, "Santa Claus had always left the North Pole with his sleigh overflowing with presents for all the children of the world."

"But in the last few years, it has gotten way too heavy!" Roxanne went on. "By the end of the trip, the reindeer were exhausted."

"The day after Christmas, the reindeer were so tired they ran a fever and had no choice but to spend the day in bed!" Robert added.

"So," Rachel chimed in, "this year, Mrs. Claus decided that things had to change. She proposed that we

ask some families from around the world for help."

"Today, for the first time in history, the reindeer will leave the North Pole with a much lighter load," Rudy explained, "and in every city they fly over, they will stop by a house and load up gifts for the neighborhood children."

"Just a minute." Little Shonda's eyes lit up. "Are you telling me that Santa Claus himself, with his sleigh and reindeer, is going to come to our house to pick up the gifts?"

"Of course!" said Romina, the smallest of the elves. She was the one who had been standing on the table in the stairwell.

"And we might get to meet him?" Manuel asked.

"If you want to, yes," Rudy answered, adjusting his round spectacles on the bridge of his nose.

The three children looked at each other with awed jubilation. They were going to see Santa! The sleigh, too! And even reindeer!

Meanwhile Rose, with her blonde pigtails, and Raphaëlle, with her long, red braid, had taken off their cone-shaped hats. In place of the hats, the two elves put on little brown helmets, and adjusted a set of aviator masks over their eyes. The lenses were sparkling and colorful.

Suddenly, a great silence came over the elves as they took each other's hands and formed a circle. They reached out and invited the children and Mama Dominique to join hands with them, too.

Roxanne declared, "It is half past nine. Our appointment with Santa Claus is exactly twelve hours from now."

"And what are we supposed to do in these twelve hours?" Camila asked shyly.

"Wrap 230,119 Christmas presents," Romina answered, checking the number on her notepad.

"We'll never be able to do that!" Mama Dominique burst out.

"Of course we'll do it, Mama," Camila said calmly. "Nothing is impossible for the Greco-Aidens!"

"But first, we have exactly one minute to lose!" Rowan said, as he pulled an elegant pocket watch out of his jacket.

"What does that mean?" Shonda asked.

"Before embarking on a difficult mission, you must lose a minute with your teammates," explained Robert, the elf with the compact black goatee and mustache. "During this minute, the elves hold hands and thank each other for sharing in a new adventure together."

"Do you want to lose a minute with us?" asked blonde-haired Raynold.

"Yes!" Camila, Shonda, Manuel, and Dominique replied enthusiastically.

Rowan set the stopwatch for sixty seconds. Everyone closed their eyes and silently, with wide open hearts, shared that mixture of gratitude, excitement, and fear that precedes the beginning of every important work.

READY, SET, GO!

As soon as the hand of the stopwatch marked the sixtieth second, Rudy whistled, and all the elves got into position. Some went to the table, others went to the boxes, still more scattered themselves around the room. Rachel opened a box labeled *ladder* and, quick as a flash, pulled out a ladder that reached right up to the dormer window.

Roxanne and Robert immediately got into position, one on the ladder and the other on the roof.

"Go!" Rudy yelled, and just like magic, an assembly chain made of ten elves, three kids, and one mom started assembling packages.

The presents were organized by category. They started with the big boxes labeled *means of transport.*

One after the other, the elves pulled out pedal cars, fire trucks, racing cars of every shape and color, vans, diggers, buses, and even some spaceships!

The toys were taken out of the boxes, put on the table to check that they weren't broken, then placed in a gift box to be wrapped, decorated with bows, and labeled with the recipient's name.

Rose and Raphaëlle were at the end of this extraordinary assembly chain. They were responsible for quality control, the most critical step of all. The goggles that they had put on before were not in fact aviator masks at all, but x-ray vision glasses that Mrs. Claus had invented herself! Once they were turned on, a fluorescent green glow emanated from the lenses and enabled anyone who was wearing them to see inside the boxes. The two elves took their responsibility very seriously, examining the packages one by one to make sure each had been wrapped with sufficient care and contained exactly what the recipient had asked for.

"Before these goggles existed," Rudy explained, "children would often find they'd been given the wrong present!"

"Once, a four-year-old girl got a tube of shaving cream that had been meant for Robert!" Roxanne blushed pink as she laughed, and all the others burst into fits of giggles.

After passing quality control, the packages were brought up to the roof, where, at exactly 9:30 p.m., Santa would pass by to pick them up. The process was so smooth, and the workers so diligent, it seemed like nothing could stop them.

THREE SUSPICIOUS NEIGHBORS

The hours flew by, and the teetering tower of packages on the roof grew taller and taller.

Everyone, including Mama Dominique, was so absorbed in the work that they didn't notice a group of people gathering in the road below their house. The people were staring up with frowning faces in the direction of their apartment.

Manuel was the first to notice.

"Mama," he said, pointing to the street corner of the house opposite their own, "what are those people doing down there, and why are they looking at our windows with those angry faces?"

Dominique looked outside: something indeed seemed terribly wrong.

"Don't worry, darling," she reassured him, "I'm going to go down right now and see what's going on. It can't be anything too serious."

Then, without even pausing to put on her jacket, she disappeared down the stairs.

As soon as she got to the road, she realized that the situation was serious indeed. With the exception of Olivia, since they had moved to R., not a single person had approached them. But the moment Dominique stepped outside, two men and a woman walked toward her.

"Do you live here, ma'am?" A gray-haired gentleman asked, pointing a finger at Dominique. Before she even had time to reply, he added, "Can you explain what is going on up there?" He tipped his gray mustache in the direction of the colorful tower of parcels piled on the roof.

"I realize that it may seem absurd, and maybe it is," Dominique began, and then told them the whole story: their move; the Flying Envelope©; the elves; the parcels; the reindeer's exhaustion; and how tiny her apartment seemed even though, in that very moment, her children and the elves were wrapping more than 200,000 presents for the children of R.

"I'm truly sorry that we disturbed you," she concluded, "but in a few hours Santa Claus is going to pass by on his sleigh to pick up the presents and take them away for delivery."

If the neighbors had seemed unfriendly before, they grew decidedly more suspicious and hostile as they listened to Dominique's story. By the end, they were outright glowering at her.

"Santa Claus?!" A woman in a fur coat, who had just come out of the hairdresser, exclaimed. "You can't be serious!"

"Yes," Dominique confirmed, "as soon as he gets here, the elves will go back to the North Pole."

"Do you think you can come here from—wherever you come from—just to make fun of us?" The woman glanced around at her neighbors for support, which they offered in the form of a chorus of angry agreement.

A young, burly man dressed in black addressed Dominique in a voice more than a little threatening. "The only reason we're even talking to you, ma'am, despite

not knowing you, is because we're very angry! How dare you answer our complaints with this load of nonsense!"

"I know it seems strange, but I can assure you that it is not nonsense," Dominique replied politely, one hand pressed to her heart as if to swear an oath. Then she had an idea. "Come up to our house! Let me make you a cup of tea, and you can see with your own eyes!"

But nobody came up. They told her that they preferred not to get involved in any way with her absurd story, and they certainly wouldn't be entering her home. They said that perhaps it was different where she came from, but in the city of R., people didn't just waltz into strangers' homes—particularly if the stranger was telling such senseless tales, thank you very much.

Dominique was mortified. She knew her story was hard to believe, but she had hoped that at least one of the neighbors would have given her the benefit of the doubt.

Instead, the gray-haired man, the woman in the fur coat, and the burly young man walked away, still talking amongst themselves. The young man had pulled out his cell phone and was dialing a number.

Who is he calling? Dominique wondered, as she closed the door to the building behind her. Then, she climbed the five flights of stairs, overwhelmed by the feeling that her neighbors were staring at her through their peepholes.

By now, the neighbors will have surely seen what happened from their windows and they will be more scared than ever! she worried to herself.

When she got up to her landing she rubbed her face with her hands. She didn't want the children to see that she was upset. Despite her efforts, Manuel knew something was wrong the moment his mother walked into the house. Camila and Shonda, however, didn't even look up, so absorbed were they in their task. They went on wrapping colorful parcels and handing them up to be stacked in towering piles on the tiled roof of the building.

"Everything is alright, darling," said Mama Dominique to her son. "How are we doing with the presents?"

"There are still 43,812 left to wrap!" Camila replied.

"We're doing well, but we have to hurry up," Rudy added. "We've only got three hours left..."

AN UNEXPECTED VISIT

There were still 10,000 presents left to wrap when a sudden loud knocking echoed from the front door.

"Police!" thundered a male voice. "Open up!" Frightened, the children and the elves all looked up at Dominique.

"Don't worry." She tried to reassure them, keeping her own fear at bay. "They're probably just checking in to see how the newcomers are doing! Maybe they want to give us an official R. welcome!"

She then took a deep breath and went to open the door. There were two policemen on the landing. The first had a big, bristly mustache and eyebrows so bushy that they nearly obscured his eyes altogether. The second,

taller man had a shock of dark hair that appeared to be doing its best to escape from beneath his uniform's neat cap. The taller policeman seemed oddly familiar to Dominique.

"Good evening, officers," Dominique said. "How can I help you?"

"Are you Mrs. Greco-Aiden?" The shorter officer seemed to be the higher-ranking of the two. His voice was grave.

"Yes, I'm Dominique Greco-Aiden."

"We received a complaint from your neighbors, ma'am," added the wild-haired officer. His eyes looked a touch kinder than his partner's, thought Dominique. "And we're required to investigate. It won't take long. Can we come in?"

"Of c-course," Dominique stammered, stalling for time, "but what was the complaint about? The elves?"

The policemen looked at her, puzzled.

"We're a bit old for believing in elves, are we not ma'am?" The officer with the mustache shook his head in disapproval, and without waiting for Dominique's permission, he marched into the apartment. His subordinate followed behind.

Dominique momentarily closed her eyes and tried to focus. *How on earth am I going to explain this?* Just as she was trying to figure out a way to account for the elves and the mountain of parcels, she noticed that the room had gone oddly quiet. Other than the creaking of the floorboards beneath the officers' slow, heavy footsteps, not a sound came from the dining room.

Dominique tiptoed cautiously into the dining room. Mere moments before, it had bustled with noise and joyful pandemonium.

Now, to her shock, she discovered that the room was completely empty; save for the old table, the five chairs, the poker, the basket of wood, and the worn carpet in front of the fireplace. Gone were the toys, the boxes, the ladder, the tape, the wrapping paper, the elves—even her own children! Dominique stood staring at the empty room. Where had everybody gone?

THE TRIP UP

"**E**verything seems to be in order to me," said the officer with the kind eyes to the serious one.

"I suppose," the mustachioed officer grumbled. Disappointed, he scoured the apartment for a clue. He'd really hoped he would find evidence of some misdeed or another. In five years, nothing bad had happened in R.—which had left the police officers very little to do.

"Great," Dominique said. She was impatient for the officers to leave, so she could figure out what had happened to her children. "Thank you for stopping by, I'll walk you to the door." As she headed toward the exit, Dominique tripped over something on the floor: a pair of x-ray gift-inspection goggles!

"And these?" asked the officer with the mustache,

triumphantly. "What, exactly, are these?" He picked the goggles up with a pencil, so as not to leave his own fingerprints on such important evidence.

"Those are..." Dominique started, scrambling for an explanation the dour officer would accept.

Just as she was trying to think of what to say, Isabella got home from work. Isabella was frightened at seeing two police officers in her home, and no children.

"Has something happened?" Isabella asked Dominique, as her heart skipped a beat.

Dominique hugged her and whispered in her ear, "Nothing serious, I think. The police arrived five minutes ago, and when they did, the children, the elves, and all the presents disappeared. Maybe they're under some kind of magic cloak."

The police officer with the mustache cleared his throat and waved the goggles to draw their attention.

Isabella had never seen the goggles before, but hoping to help her wife out of a sticky situation, she took them from the officer, put them on and said: "This is our daughter Camila's ski mask!" She blinked at the green glow emanating from the strange goggles and added, "Camila simply loves night skiing!"

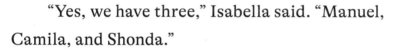

The officer with the mustache pulled a clear plastic bag out of his pocket, the kind used for collecting evidence in a crime scene, and motioned for Isabella to put the strange glasses inside. Then he glared at her. "How old is your daughter?"

"She's seven," Isabella replied proudly.

"Do you have other children?" the officer with the kind eyes asked.

"Yes, we have three," Isabella said. "Manuel, Camila, and Shonda."

"All minors?" asked the other officer, mustache bristling even more fiercely.

"Yes," Dominique replied hesitantly. She sensed this line of questioning could only lead to trouble.

"And where are they right now?" the officer demanded.

Dominique and Isabella had not the slightest idea. They knew they were in a predicament even before the mustached officer spoke the words he'd been waiting five long years to say: "You two are coming back to the station with us."

A few minutes later, Isabella and Dominique locked the door and woefully followed the mustached officer down the 104 steps, while his partner followed behind.

When they got to the police van, the officers made Dominique and Isabella get into the back seat and locked the two women in. Even the windows were armored!

The short officer slid behind the wheel, and his partner buckled himself into the passenger seat.

They had just turned onto Fingers Crossed Boulevard, when they saw a group of Scouts walking single file, snow shovels perched on their shoulders.

"Slow down, please," the kinder officer asked the one driving. "I think I saw my daughter." The chief narrowed his eyes at him: he did not want anything to delay their trip to the station.

"Please," the officer repeated.

The van pulled up to the side of the road, and the kind policeman rolled down his window. "Honey!" he shouted.

"Dad!" A little girl called back from the group of Scouts.

That bright little voice gave Isabella and Dominique a moment of hope. What they would have done to have heard their own children call out to them! Isabella and Dominique peered past the grate of the armored windows, but there was no sign of Manuel, Camila, or Shonda.

Isabella and Dominque were struck by the sharp contrast between the children, walking side by side and happily chatting to each other, and the adults who had come to pick them up. The parents didn't even get out of their cars. Instead, they stayed shut inside, windows fogging up with steam, and waited for their children to come to them. *They won't so much as get out to wish each other Happy Holidays!* Isabella thought, puzzled.

The kind officer, in the meantime, got out of the van and went to wrap his daughter in a hug. He waved back toward the policeman behind the wheel as though asking for another minute, and followed his daughter inside the Scout's clubhouse.

From within the van the mustachioed officer grunted in disapproval, while Isabella and Dominique struggled to hold back their tears.

The Scouts had been on a volunteer mission. Inside the clubhouse, they safely stowed their snow shovels in a big tool cupboard. Each Scout wore a uniform consisting of a thick, light green flannel shirt, a red neckerchief, and warm, dark green pants that puffed a little at the sides of the legs. Some of the Scouts wore beige sashes across their chests; the sashes were covered in brightly colored badges, each representing a different accomplishment.

"Look, Dad!" the little girl said, showing him her chapped hands. "I shoveled tons of snow for the elderly people at the home, and while I was there..." She reached for a mysterious object, "I invented a wrapping machine!" Olivia looked briefly disappointed. "I told them they could have it, but they didn't want it, so I brought it back with me. Watch! " Olivia's device looked as if it had been cobbled together from a drill, a bicycle wheel, a stool, a metal plate, a roll of golden ribbon, and a sheet of colored paper. The gifts the machine churned out were only

partially wrapped, but the police officer couldn't have been prouder of his daughter.

"It's wonderful!" he told her. "But we have to go home now. My partner is waiting outside in the van."

The little girl picked up the device, dismantling it as she followed her father.

"Good evening, Olivia!" The officer with the mustache sounded as if he did not hope she had a good evening at all.

Isabella and Dominique looked at each other in shock. Had the officer said, "Olivia"? Could she possibly be the same Olivia with the Motocase? The one who had left the message in the bottle?

The little girl sat down next to her father and cheerfully greeted the mustached officer, ignoring his bitter tone. She didn't seem to notice the two women in the back seat. But as soon as Isabella and Dominique saw that it truly was her, they squeezed each others' hands, feeling again a glimmer of hope.

ON THE WAY TO THE STATION

Shortly after they had gotten under way, Olivia noticed Isabella and Dominique seated in the back of the van. As her eyes met theirs, she was taken by surprise, but she quickly turned to face front and pretended that she had not recognized them.

"We're going to drop you off at the house with Mom, and I'll see you when I get home for dinner, all right?" the kind officer asked Olivia.

The driver snorted and shook his head in protest, but didn't say anything.

With studied casualness, Olivia asked her father, "Why? Where are you going?"

"To the police station, honey," he replied.

"Have these ladies done something serious?" Olivia

asked, lowering her voice.

"Nothing for you to worry about! They lost track of their kids so we need to make sure everything is alright."

"We didn't 'lose track of them,'" Dominique protested. "They were home with me, as well as the ten elves!"

Dominique told the officers the tale: the second letter to Santa; how her children had asked for a CB radio; Santa's reply; the Flying Envelope©; their house which had magically grown bigger; the 230,119 Christmas presents; the 9:30 p.m. deadline; and the inexplicable disappearance of the elves, the children and everything to do with the presents the moment the policemen had set foot in their house.

Dominique admitted that she did not, in fact, know where her children were at that moment, but she had certainly not 'lost track of them.' She added that wherever they might be, she was sure the elves were with them.

"Still telling the 'elves' story, eh, ma'am?" the officer behind the wheel sneered.

As soon as Olivia heard the story, a look of

excited amazement came over her face. *What an incredible family!* she thought to herself. *The moment I saw those kids, I knew they were special... I really want to help them!*

The engine sputtered in the cold, and it seemed to the two moms that even the van was coughing skeptically at Dominique's story.

Dismayed, they looked at each other. Dominique and Isabella had dropped everything and left their home country in order to keep their family safe—away from jails, prisons, orphanages, and guards—and, more than anything, to never be apart. They'd only been in R. a few days, and they had already ended up locked in the back of an armored police van—with no sign of their children.

Dominique stared out the window. It was dark, and the snow had started up again. She could see lights come on in windows as people in their homes prepared to celebrate Christmas.

Isabella put her arm around Dominique's shoulder. "Everything is going to be okay, my love," she whispered. Her wife raised her eyes and stroked Isabella's cheek.

The silence was broken by the kind officer, who told his partner, "Take a right turn and then head left, and we'll drop Olivia off. Our place is 1 Heroines Who Save the Day Way."

A LEAD
TO FOLLOW

The van stopped, and the kind-eyed police officer helped his daughter out. She grabbed the pieces of her gift-wrapping machine and took off toward her house. Her father blew a kiss after her.

"Let's hope the elves don't make you disappear, too!" the serious officer joked, and laughed hard enough to shake the springs in his leather seat.

When the little Scout got to her front door, she turned. Before going inside, Olivia locked eyes with Isabella, who was staring out the window. Did Isabella imagine it, or was the girl trying to tell her something? Olivia stared at her intensely for a few seconds, then smiled and disappeared behind the heavy front door.

They watched from the street as the light in one of

the rooms inside the building turned on. Two seconds later, Olivia appeared and waved to her father from the window so that he would know that she had arrived safely. "Always cautious!" He often told her, doing his best to teach her how to be a good citizen of R.

Olivia had replied the same way every time, since the age of three: "Adventure always!" The little girl watched as the police van slipped and slid through the light of the streetlamps, all the way down the snowy road toward the station.

"It's 8:01," Olivia said to herself. "From what their mother said, Santa Claus is going to get there in less than an hour and a half."

She sat down at her desk, opened her diary and wrote, in her very best handwriting, "The Mysterious Case of the Elves on the Fifth Floor."

There, she wrote down Dominique's entire tale, word for word. Then she circled everything that seemed important with a colored marker: *radio, Flying Envelope*©, *presents, ladder, roof, neighbors, Santa Claus, police...*

Think, Olivia, think, she told herself. *How would*

you disappear from a fifth-floor apartment? You'd have to go down the stairs—or climb across the rooftops...

Could they have escaped by way of the roof? *To go where?* Olivia picked up her map of the city and saw that the roof of 10 Roomy Chimneys Road, bordered that of an old abandoned building at the corner of Fake Clues Alley. It would be the perfect hiding place, and relatively easy to reach from the nearby roof. Olivia examined the narrow alleyway with a magnifying glass.

"Either way, it's a lead," she said aloud, "and the only one I have at the moment, so I better follow it! But not by myself..."

She put on her helmet, gloves, and motorcycle goggles, and, taking care not to let her mom hear her, snuck down to the garage. There, her trusty four-seater sled was waiting for her. It was flaming red and studded with white stars, with long wooden rails and an electric motor connected to two huge fans in the back.

Olivia placed the pieces of her new wrapping machine under her seat and climbed aboard. There was a radio in the centre of the dashboard, which Olivia

immediately tuned to channel 38B. A brief metallic screech echoed from the speaker.

"Code Purple. All units respond. Code Purple," Olivia called.

After a burst of noise, the crackling sound of a child's voice came through: "Pablo here, over." A few seconds later, another voice: "Aisha here, over." And then another: "Tom here, over."

Olivia repeated: "Code Purple. I'm picking you up in four minutes and three seconds. Meet in Possible Missions Square. Over and out."

Then she flicked the ignition switch, and set off.

A few blocks away, on a sidewalk facing a fountain with frozen water, three children stood waiting. All were dressed in Scout uniforms, neckerchiefs tied smartly.

As soon as Olivia pulled up, Pablo asked, "Code Purple?! What happened?"

"I'll tell you everything on the way," Olivia cut him off, and motioned for the kids to climb onto the sled.

Pablo, Aisha, and Tom climbed aboard, and the sled shot away with a lurch, toward 10 Roomy Chimneys Road.

THE GREEN RIBBON

When they got there, Olivia parked the sled on the side of the road and waited with her friends for someone to come out of the building so that they could sneak inside. Once past the door, they made their way to the top of the stairs, to the fifth-floor apartment where the Greco-Aidens lived.

Aisha unhooked a pin from her Scout neckerchief and told the others: "At the count of three, shake the door as hard as you can!"

She then very carefully inserted the pin into the key-hole. Instead of counting up, she simply shouted, "Three!"

Aisha was like that: she loved acting impulsively, but her friends knew that and loved her for it. They were always sure to be ready for the unexpected. At her signal, they began shaking the old door as hard as they could.

To Aisha's satisfaction, the door opened right away.

Once inside the apartment, Pablo, Tom, and Aisha began looking around, while Olivia went into the dining room to find the window that would lead to the roof.

"There's no ladder," she observed. "Let's get the rope." Tom retrieved a climbing rope from his backpack. It had a hook attached to one end. He swung it up toward the ceiling, anchoring it to one of the beams next to the window. As quick as squirrels, the four Scouts scampered up one after the other. In no time at all, they were on the roof.

"That way, hurry!" Olivia said, shining her flashlight toward the building at the corner of Fake Clues Alley. The building was abandoned, weedy, and crumbling; it gave everyone the creeps. The brave children snuck into the first apartment through a worm-eaten balcony. They scoured the dark and damp building floor-by-floor, but found no trace of elves, children, parcels, x-ray goggles, or anything from the fantastic story Olivia had told them during the sleigh ride.

When they eventually got back inside Manuel, Camila, and Shonda's dining room, Olivia noticed that Pablo had a green ribbon in his hand.

"Where did you get that?" she asked.

"It was on the roof, on top of the chimney. I took it for my little sister. Why?"

What was a gift ribbon doing on top of the chimney?

Olivia, turned toward Aisha, radiant. "Are you thinking what I'm thinking?" she asked the other girl.

"Roomy Chimneys Road!" Aisha replied. "Of course! How come we didn't think of that before?!"

It was 9:05. In twenty-five minutes, Santa would be there.

The four children ran to the fireplace and peered up the chimney, but it was pitch dark, and they could see nothing.

They took their neckerchiefs and tied them across their mouths and noses. They looked like a gang of robbers from the Wild West.

"Quick! Lift me up onto your shoulders!" Pablo ordered Aisha. He climbed up and reached inside the chimney, feeling around with his hands. "I feel a bow!" He yelled. "And here's a boot!" And then, "This is an elbow!"

"Pull! Pull!" Olivia, Tom, and Aisha shouted, while holding Pablo's legs very tightly.

With a roar, an avalanche of elves, children, and presents tumbled into the room—along with a cloud of black soot. For a second, no one could see anything, and only the sound of coughing could be heard. Then, the soot began to settle, and the elves and children clambered out from beneath the mountain of parcels. A thick layer of black dust covered them, from the tips of their ears right down to their toes.

Shonda was the first to speak, "Where are our mommies?" she asked, looking around the room.

"Your mommies are perfectly safe!" Olivia replied. "They sent me here to help you deliver the presents to Santa Claus. They'll be back soon."

Tom and Aisha were doing their best to distinguish children from elves beneath layers of soot.

"Olivia?!" Manuel exclaimed, recognizing the girl's voice, despite the thick dust.

"Hi, you must be Manuel!" she said, taking the neckerchief off her face. "These are my friends, Aisha, Tom, and Pablo."

Camila spoke up next. "Nice to meet you! I'm Camila," she introduced herself. "This is Shonda. And they," she said, pointing to the elves, "are Rudy, Robert, Rose, Raphaëlle, Roxanne, Rachel, Roy, Raynold, Romina, and Rowan."

"Thank you for setting us free!" Romina sighed, shaking the soot off her pointed hat.

"The hiding place worked..." observed Rose, whose idea it had been.

"If only we hadn't gotten stuck, it would have been perfect!" Rudy commented, stretching his back.

As soon as Rowan was able to clean off his pocket watch, he exclaimed: "It's 9:11! We'll never be able to get all these presents ready in time for Santa! Look, they are filthy!"

But Manuel, Camila, and Shonda had promised to complete the mission, no matter what.

"Of course we will!" Camila said, smiling at Rowan, "but first we have to lose a minute."

The children and elves held hands and welcomed their four new friends into the circle to express their gratitude in sharing a new challenge together. At the sixtieth second, though their faces were still as dusty as ever, their minds were clear.

"We have to go and get the sled!" Olivia said so confidently that no one raised an objection. They all raced down, and together they were able to heave the sled up the 104 steps in less than three minutes.

Once they had it inside the apartment, Olivia got to work. With the help of her imagination and a handy screwdriver, she turned the huge fans mounted on the back of the sled until they faced toward the middle of the room.

"Hold on tight!" she warned.

This time, when Olivia flicked the ignition switch, a strong wind began to blow. For a moment, everyone was afraid that the building itself might take off into the air, but soon the windows flew wide open, and the wind carried the soot off of everyone's hair, faces, shoes, and clothing in a magnificent and silent explosion.

NINE-THIRTY

Now that the parcels were as good as new, the elves once again formed a chain to relay presents up to the roof, while the children finished wrapping the remaining packages.

Luckily, Olivia had brought her wrapping machine on the back of the sled! Its results weren't always the best, but seeing as how they had very little time, it was better than nothing.

They were the perfect team: Camila held the list of presents, Shonda picked up the toy, Pablo put it in the box, and Manuel positioned it on the wrapping machine. When the present came out on the other side, Aisha yelled "Three!" and tossed the gift to Rudy, who passed it up the ladder to the other elves; and from there, it was added to the pile on the roof.

Every so often, the device would jam and needed a squirt of oil, a little tap, or a screw tightened, and Olivia and Tom would fix it.

At 9:28 Aisha yelled, "Three!" and threw the last parcel up to Rudy.

They had done it!

They all hurried up the ladder and onto the roof to wait for Santa Claus.

It had stopped snowing. The sky was clear, and the rooftops of the city of R. sparkled in the moonlight. It was very cold, but the excited children barely noticed the chill: they were about to meet Santa Claus.

At 9:29, Olivia, Manuel, Tom, Shonda, Pablo, Camila, and Aisha took each others' hands. A few seconds later they heard the far-off sound of hoofbeats, and a loud voice exclaimed, "Ho ho ho!"

And then it was 9:30. The children followed the sound of jingling bells; and there, against the moon, they spotted the unmistakable silhouette of Santa Claus's sleigh, pulled by eight magnificent reindeer. What a sight! As they approached, the children rubbed their eyes, scarcely believing that they were finally seeing what they had before only imagined: the soft white fur that edged Santa's clothes, reins firmly grasped in red gloves, the reindeer's beautiful harnesses, and the red and gold sleigh shining in the moonlight.

"Woah!" Santa Claus called gently to his reindeer, as they landed on the roof of 10 Roomy Chimneys Road.

"Good evening, children!" Santa looked at Shonda, Olivia, Tom, Pablo, Aisha, Manuel, and Camila, each in turn. "And thank you so much for your help! Without you, not one child of R. would have received a single present this Christmas!"

Next, he turned to the elves. "Good evening, elves! I see you've been as industrious and inventive as always!" Santa told them, smiling.

The elves loaded up the sleigh at lightning speed.

Santa Claus was about to take the reins and leave, when Olivia leaned in close to him and whispered something in his ear. Santa Claus nodded, then took off into the sky.

DOCTOR PHONEY

L oaded up with presents, the sleigh flew over the chimney tops and disappeared into the night. It had started snowing again. Everyone climbed back down the ladder and into the house. Once they were inside, Rudy whistled, and the elves began gathering up the materials that had been left over from their incredible feat.

"Are you leaving right away?" Shonda asked, a bit sad. She was tired, and she had begun to miss her mothers.

"Yes, unfortunately..." said Raphaëlle. "Tomorrow we have to be at the North Pole in time for Christmas dinner!"

"Would you mind leaving the table and chairs, please?" asked Olivia.

"Of course not! We'd be happy to leave them to thank you for your hospitality and help!" Rudy agreed. The elves finished collecting their things, hugged the children, then hopped down the stairs as quick as bunnies.

"What are we going to do with such a long table, and all these chairs?" wondered Manuel. "There are only the three of us celebrating Christmas this year. We don't even have our mothers!"

"Don't worry!" Olivia said. Then she motioned for Tom, Pablo, and Aisha to come closer. The four kids squeezed into a circle and conferred for a couple of minutes. When they parted, it was clear that they had a plan.

"Can we use the phone?" Olivia asked.

"Sure!" Camila replied.

Tom picked up the phone, covered the mouthpiece of the receiver with a tissue, and dialed a number: his own home.

"Hello?" He spoke with the serious voice of an adult with a very bad cold. "My name is Doctor Phoney. I'm calling because your son, Tom, is not feeling at all well. I rescued him from the road outside and brought him home to my apartment so he could warm up. There's no way he can go home by himself, so you're going to need to come and get him. Unfortunately he's very weak, but in my super-specialized, multi-degreed medical opinion, he just might avoid mortal consequences if he were to immediately eat the chocolate cake that you made for dessert. Hurry!" He then gave them the address and hung up.

He repeated the call three more times—to Olivia's mom, one of Aisha's dads, and Pablo's dad and asked them to bring a spinach pie, baked pasta, and a roast.

"Shall we set the table?" Tom proposed, after finishing the last call. The children got to work, making use of whatever odds and ends they could find in the house. They made decorations from the leftover ribbons and scraps of wrapping paper that the elves had left behind. The end result was a beautiful, festive table that any family would be proud of.

But this was not enough to cheer Manuel, Camila, and Shonda up. They still didn't know where their mothers were, nor when they'd be back.

Olivia noticed. "I promise your moms will celebrate

Christmas Eve with us tonight. Trust me, it's all going to be perfect."

As soon as she finished saying those words, the doorbell rang. Pablo looked out the window: it was Aisha's dads. A few steps behind came Tom's mom and dad, and right behind them, his own dad and little sister! The plan had worked! Each of the guests held in their hands one of the dishes specifically requested by Doctor Phoney.

MERRY CHRISTMAS!

When Tom, Aisha, Olivia, and Pablo's parents got to the top of the 104 steps and reached the fifth floor, they immediately understood that their children had played a joke on them, and that Doctor Phoney—true to his name—did not, in fact, exist. They didn't have the slightest idea why they had been dragged there, and they wanted to leave as soon as possible. The adults of the city of R. weren't used to being together. They were afraid that people who were not immediate family members could be a threat to the safe, insulated life that they had strived to build, and so they tried to keep interaction with strangers to the absolute minimum.

"Shall we go?" Olivia's mother asked abruptly. "Dad will be home soon. This Christmas Eve has already been busy enough, don't you think?"

"Get moving!" One of Aisha's dads snapped. "We'll talk about this when we get home!"

"Shame on you!" Pablo's dad said angrily, grabbing his son by the arm. "You almost gave me a heart attack!"

"Do you think this is funny?" Tom's mother said, threateningly.

At this point, Manuel stepped forward and said, "We are very sorry that you got a fright. But tonight, we all worked together to save Christmas for the kids of R. My sisters and I wouldn't have been able to do it on our own, but thanks to your children, we succeeded." He then told the whole tale of what had happened.

"Olivia, Tom, Pablo, and Aisha are heroes!" Camila said. "Please don't be angry at them."

"The reason they asked you to come here tonight with food is because they didn't want us to be alone on Christmas Eve. Our mommies aren't here, and we don't know where they are," Shonda explained, her voice trembling as she tried to hold back tears.

The adults all looked at each other: they knew

that they could not leave the three children on their own. Pablo's father was the first one to break the ice by asking Olivia's mother for her spinach pie recipe. Then, Olivia's mom complimented Tom's mother on her beautiful dress. One of Aisha's dads told a joke to Pablo's little sister, who broke into a fit of giggles so contagious that they all couldn't help but smile.

Little by little, they all began to chat with one another: they'd forgotten what a pleasure it was to spend time together. Someone turned on the oven to heat up the roast, someone else sliced the bread, another yet uncorked a bottle of wine; and without even realizing what they were doing, they found themselves all happily seated at the table together.

It was then that they noticed the four empty chairs.

"Who are these for?" Camila asked, motioning to the chairs.

She had not even finished asking the question when they heard the familiar jingling of bells and approaching hoofbeats, followed by an unmistakable voice: "Ho ho ho!"

Everyone jumped up and rushed to the window. Beyond the glass, they could see Santa Claus and his flaming red sleigh. But next to him sat Olivia's dad; and in the back, seated tightly together, were none other than Isabella and Dominique! Their faces were full of wonder, as if they couldn't believe they were flying over the city on Santa's sleigh!

"Mommy! Mama!" Shonda cried out.

"My darlings!" Isabella and Dominique called back.

Quick as a flash, the sleigh landed on the rooftop. The mothers jumped down and hurried to hug their children.

Olivia's dad and Santa Claus followed them inside. The spot at the head of the table was saved for Santa himself.

Before sitting down, Santa raised his glass in the air. Everyone grew quiet as he toasted: "To friendship in the city of R., and to the courage to open your homes and your hearts to those we do not yet know!"

Everyone clinked glasses and cheered: "Merry Christmas!"

"Merry Christmas," Santa said. "Ho ho ho!"

THE END

Heartfelt Gratitude Alley

Thanks to the cold and gray month of May that Rome gave me, and to the attic in Trastevere where I wrote the first draft of this story. Thanks to my sister, my parents, my cousins, and my aunts: your affection crosses oceans and finds me wherever I may be, like a cozy fire that always makes me feel safe. Thanks to Samuele, for the combination of affection and extraordinary talent you have put in every project we have worked on for the last ten years. Thanks to Verena, for throwing yourself into this book with such enormous enthusiasm, infinite patience, and humility. Thanks to Silvia, Gaia, Raffaele, Luca, Stéphanie, and Anna, for being close to me when I needed it most.

Thank you to all the little and big readers that came and met me all over the world, and to everyone who wrote with thanks, encouragement, or even just a hello. Telling stories that fill your hearts is the greatest privilege of my life. Thanks to Emilio: your arrival in my life has reminded me of the things that really matter.

Little Biographies Lane

 **FRANCESCA CAVALLO** is a *New York Times* bestselling author, entrepreneur, and activist born in Taranto (Italy) in 1983. She is the co-author of the "Good Night Stories for Rebel Girls" book series and podcast, and the co-founder of the company who gave birth to the project, Timbuktu Labs. In 2018, she won the *Publishers Weekly* Star Watch Award. In 2019, she parted ways with Rebel Girls to start Undercats, Inc. with the mission to radically increase diversity in children's media. Cavallo's books have been translated into more than 50 languages and have sold more than 5 million copies worldwide.

Francesca lives in Rome with a cat named Dopamina.

Instagram @francescatherebel

 **VERENA WUGEDITSCH** is a young Austrian illustrator. She lives in the small village of Sankt Andrä-Wördern, where she studies graphic and communication design. *Elves on the Fifth Floor* is her first book.

Instagram @verenart

Spreaders of Good News Square

If you enjoyed this book, please tell your friends about it, review it online, or write a post on social media using the hashtag **#ElvesontheFifthFloor** and tagging **@undercatsmedia**. In short, do not keep it to yourself: we are committed to making children's books that make the world a more inclusive place, but we can't do it without your help.

One Last Thing
Boulevard

Undercats is a small, independent publisher with a big mission: radically increase diversity in children's media and inspire families around the world to take action for equality. We are a female led, LGBTQ+ owned company with a very diverse team spread across two continents.

If you liked this book, you may like these other books we published:

www.undercats.com

"Goodnight Tonight" is our newsletter. Sign up if you want to receive free bedtime stories celebrating some of the most beautiful things happening in the world right now.

www.undercats.com/goodnight

Instagram @undercatsmedia
Twitter @undercatsmedia